A CHS Test® production:
www.chstest.com

THE BURDEN

Dedicated to my beloved family & friends

Written by: Istvan Szabo

Cover Design: Muhammad Fermli

Interior Design: Muhammad Fermli

Publisher: CHS Test®

Editor: Stephanie Brush

Creative Consultant: Stephanie Brush

Consciousness = Happiness + Self-confidence
www.chstest.com

CHAPTERS

CHAPTER I – AN UNEXPECTED CHALLENGE

Once upon a time there was a farmer and his wife in the fertile Shinmara province, in a distant land. They had five children; three sons and two daughters and they lived in harmony with many animals on a peaceful farm. The youngest boy – Chon – had just turned twelve years old. He was a very kind boy, reliable, hardworking and silent compared to all the other children. He always found time to play with the animals on the farm. Often, they followed him until he finally stopped and petted them. His mother loved him more than anything, and always used to tell him that he would one day be a great man, well-known in the whole country. Chon did not entirely believe her, but he smiled because he was the happiest boy on the world in the aura of his loving mother.

On a late autumn day, the farmer summoned his children and announced the following:

"My children, the walnuts are now ripe. As you know, we have to sell them in the neighbouring Dar-Lan province which is thirty days' walking distance from us. The route leading there presents many potential dangers. Still we have to undertake this journey because we have to buy firewood with the money received for this particularly precious product. This year, who will deliver it to Mr. Hano, our trader, who will buy them for a fair price?"

All his children volunteered for the mission – except young Chon.

"No, my children, you have already all accomplished this journey," said the farmer, then continued. "This year, I would like young Chon to haul the walnuts to Mr. Hano. None of you have undertaken this serious mission at such a young age, but I am convinced that Chon is ripe enough for it." The farmer delivered his message with compassion but with a strictness that tolerated no contradiction.

Young Chon knew that it was the ultimate decision, and thus, irrevocable. Although he had never been beyond the boundaries of his farm, the unknown skyline had always attracted him. He trusted his father and knew that he would never give him a task that was too big to cope with. Therefore, he set off the next day at dawn, and put on his back the bag full of walnuts, which was not much smaller than he was himself. He felt his father's gaze on him and it permeated his heart with immense pride.

CHAPTER II – THE TRIAL OF STRENGTH

When he set off, a little bird started to follow him and when Chon slowed down the colorful bird landed on a rock or a branch and started to sing. Chon carried the burden with overwhelming enthusiasm. He knew that the road was long, but it did not matter. This first journey in his life filled his being with mysterious excitement. He was finally part of something important. He was contributing to the family, and that was a serious challenge.

At the boundaries of the farm, he sighed, looked around and gladly progressed on his way. It was the beginning of a fabulous autumn day with the scents of joy in the air. The rising sun was playfully warming up the meadows beyond the farm with its teasing rays. The gravel road led through rolling hills, crossed the Green River with a small stone bridge, and then disappeared in the endless distance. Here and there, trees and groves rimmed the landscape. On the far horizon, the contours of the Big Peaky Mountain rose into the clouds. On the other side of the mountain was Dar-Lan province where Mr. Hano lived.

The farmer had briefly advised young Chon about the mission. He said that the road led over the Big Peaky Mountain, straight to the bustling village of Mr. Hano in Dar-Lan province. He also strongly advised Chon not to stop and not to veer from the road; otherwise there would be no time to return before winter set in.

He did not reveal what difficulties could occur, how Chon could cope with those difficulties, where and how he could get food, who could help him in need, where he could sleep when the sun sets, and how he should behave with bandits and other bad people. He did not say how he could distinguish those who would help him from those who would want to take advantage of him. Young Chon took the task seriously, and wholeheartedly believed that he could accomplish it. He had no idea, however, of the vast scale of the challenge. For his own relief he repeated the parting words of his father:

"Follow the path, my son. Over Big Peaky Mountain, you will find the village where Mr. Hano will already be waiting for you. You need to deliver the bag of walnuts to him and in return, he will pay you its price. You have to bring the money back to us so that we can buy firewood before winter. If you deviate from the road, you can't get back before winter, and you will freeze, as will we. Here you are: a few coins and a bundle of food. This will hold you for a while if you consume it consciously."

The first day, Chon proceeded without stopping. He did not even pause for lunch so as not to lose any time. He carried the heavy burden on his back the whole day. The little bird that had joined him when he set off miraculously accompanied him the whole way. By the end of the day, when Chon stopped at the bank of the Green River, his legs were trembling, his shoulders and neck hurt as never before, and his whole body was stiff and in pain. In just the course of a single day, he had reached the maximum limit of his physical capacity, and – he thought – he could not move anymore even if he were threatened with punishment. His hands were in a state of cramp as a consequence of holding the heavy burden through the entire day. Worst of all was that – as he saw it – the silhouette of Big Peaky Mountain had not gotten at all closer after the day-long march.

A dense night soon covered the beautiful landscape, transforming it into a different, threatening place. The first night was terrible. As Chon writhed sleeplessly, he became gradually convinced that he could not accomplish the difficult task. The first day had been so devastating that he thought that he could not ever walk through another day. The whole distance ahead of him seemed utterly impossible. The dark night loomed over an eerie landscape. Chon had never felt so alone and so desperate. He started to play with the thought that he would leave the burden there, and the next day, return home. By morning, he could already be home, and the next evening he would already be sleeping under his soft blanket. Then, immediately he remembered his father – as he looked into his eyes compassionately but rigorously. He knew that if he returned, he would lose his trust forever.

He sighed and shook his head. This was a test, his first test. If he failed, he would never be able to wash the shame off his face. He realized that he could not return, and this journey was not going to be a simple journey but a life-and-death struggle, from which he would either return gloriously, or die. There was no way back. He had to move forward.

He woke up tired and sleepy the next morning. The unknown place, the strange sounds of nature all around, and the emotional burden of his task all prevented him from sleeping deeply. He only became relieved when he again saw his companion the little bird who started to sing joyfully with the first rays of the morning sun. Even though his limbs were heavy and his hunger and thirst were unbearable, he did not want to turn back anymore. In his strong heart he knew what he was supposed to do, so he tried to avoid the alarming thoughts dissuading him from his mission. He bit from the bread in his bundle packed by his father, sipped from his canteen, then set off. A sort of unearthly force pulled him onto the road again, irresistibly. When he started to walk he realized, not with small surprise, that he was able to make some progress.

Though it was much harder than the previous day, when he'd set off with enthusiasm, at least he was able to walk, and that realization comforted him. There was an enormous distance ahead of him, but he tried to avoid thinking about the journey beyond those few meters which he could see before the next turn. In that moment it was enough that he could continue walking.

He alleviated his hunger with the fruits from the orchards along the way, and he drank from a spring from which he also filled his canteen. With strong concentration, he managed not to think of the future and the vast distance ahead. He knew what was expected from him in the present moment, and he did it. Being present in the given moment increased his strength and relieved his pain, even though the bag of walnuts was as heavy as before. Stress is inherently rooted in a focus on the future and in the realization of how difficult a certain task ahead of us is, and how weak we may be. Chon did not think of anything on that harmoniously improving morning other than the next step ahead of him. The heavy weight hurt him, and he progressed much more slowly than on the previous day…but he was on his way, going straight ahead. Inside his mind, he put away the thought that there were still twenty-nine days of walking, and he believed that the success of the project depended on his good fortune. He only had to focus on the present and do what he was capable of in the given moment. His focus was on something much simpler than succeeding at the whole task, he simply concentrated on each step he was taking, one at a time. This increased his awareness and helped him move forward. At noon he stopped, sat down, and leaned his back against the trunk of a big old tree. The little bird sat above him on a branch. It had never dared to get so close to Chon before. "What is your name, my little friend?" asked the boy and offered it a small piece of bread. After it timidly took the bread, Chon sipped from his canteen with pleasure and took his modest lunch from the bundle.

He was entirely content, and enjoyed sitting. As he looked around, it comforted him that he had already progressed despite his terrible morning. Looking back on the road, the contours of his farm faded in the far distance. There was no doubt anymore: He was on his way! It did not matter how hard it was; he decided that he was not going to think of returning. Even though he did not see the end of the road, and could not even imagine how distant it was, he longed to carry the weight on to his destination.

In early afternoon he set off again. The little bird flew high ahead of him, as if leading him on his way. This departure was again an extremely hard one. The rays of the sun languidly caressed the tired boy.

He knew that he could not stop, and he could not enjoy the breathtaking beauty and sweet harmony of the landscape. Even if a moment might be extremely tempting to prolong, it could sometimes be a mere illusion; a stolen bit of harmony which would only divert us from our goal. Young Chon knew that he had to progress on his journey or he would not be able to accomplish his goal and deliver the walnuts to Mr. Hano. So, he continued walking with the bag of walnuts on his back straight along the road. By the road there were immense meadows edged with a few trees and with huge freestanding rocks. There was glorious sunshine, and only a few fluffy clouds hung in the sky.

As a consequence of the unchanging landscape, young Chon started to be more and more tired. His thoughts wandered again into the future. He could only think of his rest at the end of the day…but it was still too far. He was sweating freely, felt no strength in his legs anymore and his entire body was shaking from the unbearable pain. He realized that it was only the second day, and he was not going to be able to make the whole journey.

He again started to think about how he could explain to his father that he could not deliver the walnuts to their destination. Maybe he would say that they were stolen…"Yes, this is a good idea!" surged into his mind, but as soon as he formulated the thought, he felt ashamed. "I could not lie to my father," he knew. In the meantime, the weight became more and more unbearable. He continued on with his train of thoughts. He considered that he would not even return home. He would be fine alone in nature! How lovely it would be to just wander without the burden on his back! He would not need anyone else. As he was thinking about all this, he diverted his concentration from his task, the straps of his bag became loose and suddenly the whole bag of walnuts fell off his back and it spilled out its contents until every last walnut lay on the road, or in the meadow along the road.

As he realized what he had done, he collapsed and started to cry. This incident brought him back from wondering and into the present moment.

He was shaking, entirely lost. Even his little companion had disappeared.

"At least somebody should be here, who would listen to me…somebody who would tell me what to do, who would look into my eyes, pat me on my shoulders and tell that I can do this!" he thought desperately.

In that instant, he realized that he could not do this alone. He had not progressed much during the day, and now he had to pause again, and on top of everything else, the walnuts were everywhere on the road. Maybe he would not even find them all, and maybe pests would destroy them if he did not collect them in time. But he could not even think of collecting the walnuts at that moment. He was in a state of collapse. Even when he stopped crying, an extreme tiredness started to cast a spell upon him.

He had been just sitting there, staring into nothingness for an hour already. He was frowning, and gazing at the endless road ahead of him with his big black eyes. His situation seemed impossible. He knew that he could not go back, but he also knew that he could not cope with the burden. Then, suddenly, from deep inside him, a voice started to speak, slowly, with compassion, but rigorously, as his father had used to speak:

"You have to continue! You can do it!"

As he looked up, he noticed that an ox-hauled wagon was approaching with a peasant who ostensibly was just making an ordinary trip back to his village. The little bird was sitting on top of the ox's head. The ox was strolling unhurriedly. His big horns reached majestically into the air, and seemingly he did not care that a bird was atop him. As they drew next to Chon, the peasant cried out:

"What are you doing here young man with that immense bag and those walnuts on the road?"

"I am carrying them to Dar-Lan province as requested by my father."

"Oooh, crazy boy…Do you know how far that is? You are still too small to undertake such a journey alone…but if you are already here – " sigh – "I can take you to the next junction. From there, I will need to go to Halung to the west, and you will need to continue towards the Big Peaky Mountain."

Chon nodded, mesmerized, and could only whisper a "thank you" that was almost inaudible. Then the peasant jumped off the cart, righted the bag and vigorously started to collect the walnuts into it. As Chon saw this, he also started to collect them, with gradually increasing happiness. As he collected them one by one, his sense of mission regained its power again.

He was careful not to step on any of them and not to put any other waste into the bag which could then contaminate the prime contents. He was entirely focused on his task. First, he collected them in his hands, and when he could not carry any more, he put them into the bag. He started to collect the walnuts from the road, then from the grass along the road. As the bag filled up, he became saturated with energy, purpose and life again. Not much later, the bag was full because both of them were working on it. Thus, it was much easier and faster. Eventually, the peasant put the bag in the back of the cart and they set off together.

As they sat silently next to each other, Chon was deeply submerged in his thoughts. The peasant's words echoed in his mind: That he was too small for this task. "Should I not have tried to dissuade my father?" Although, somehow, he felt that the decision about his journey had already been made. The task was exciting. It was something he had not experienced before. It gave him an opportunity to show what he was capable of.

He felt joy. And that joy was different from those temporal joys he had felt before, when he had been playing childish pranks, or when he was recognized because he had cleaned up his belongings. This was rooted much deeper and was permeated with creative energy. He was sure that while he was on the road, this sensation of contentment and usefulness, resulting from his focus on his mission, would accompany him. He looked back.

"What an immense burden," he sighed. At the same time, he thought proudly that this burden meant his entire life at the moment. If he managed to deliver it to Dar-Lan province, and to bring back the money to his father, he would surely be respectfully recognized. The whole family would be proud of him, and he would be the first one to complete this journey so young. God only knew what amazing miracles would still be ahead of him.

The journey with the peasant concluded shortly because they arrived at the junction where the boy had to get off. From this point, Chon continued to travel alone in the ensuing days, straight ahead, always toward the distant Big Peaky Mountain which were on the way to Dar-Lan. One gloomy morning, in the course of many long exhausting days of marching, it seemed to Chon as if his energy level had started to rise.

More and more often an immense joy saturated his heart, which then permeated his body with a sense of endurance. Sometimes hours passed without seeming exertion as he just gazed at the beauty of the landscape and realized that Big Peaky Mountain definitely looked closer than before. It was almost right in front of him.

CHAPTER III – THE TRIAL OF MIND

The way, however, still led through Daze-Stone City before going over the Big Peaky Mountain. Chon had never seen such a big city. Along the streets, covered with paving stones, multi-story buildings reared. Small streets streamed into bigger ones and those ended up at the main square of the city, where the famous Daze-Stone Temple stood serenely.

The night was already falling when Chon trudged through the sparkling city with the immense bag on his back. He progressed on his way as before, paying attention to his purest inner voice. This terrain, however, was different from everything else he had experienced earlier. In nature he already knew which fruits were edible, where he could find clean water and how he could build a shelter. Here in Daze-Stone City his survival instincts were useless. His focus was scattered.

He passed by a tavern from which he heard live music, and the voices of people arguing and laughing. Not much further a woman leaned against a wall. Her short skirt unveiled her beautiful long legs. She had long black hair and exaggerated make-up. She did not take her teasing eyes from the boy approaching in her direction on the road. She smiled and winked when Chon passed by. Then he saw groups of men along the road, playing cards or gambling. They looked at the young boy occasionally. Sometimes they said something to each other, looked at Chon again, and laughed scornfully.

The boy contemplated this pulsating life around him with amazement. He started to feel his bag as a burden again. Rather than physical, though, this was a different type of burden. It was a painful commitment to complete a task, which he now experienced as a captivity, paralyzing him and limiting his freedom to enjoy his life on a full scale. For a moment he started to play with the idea of selling the walnuts in that city and doubling his fortune by gambling. Euphoric joy took control of him when he imagined how happy his father would be if he arrived earlier and with more money than expected. In addition, he could spend a few days in the city in a comfortable hotel, having good food and, finally, a warm bath.

As he was cheering himself up with these thoughts, he felt the burden grow even more uncomfortable. He realized that in the city nobody resembled him. Their style, their dress, and their behavior were completely different. He was ashamed and wanted to be invisible. Worst of all was that he did not even see his little bird friend anywhere since he had arrived in the city.

Suddenly a kind-faced middle-aged woman stepped up to Chon with a friendly smile:

"Good evening young man. Where are you heading to with that immense bag?"

"I need to deliver this bag full of walnuts to Dar-Lan province, to Mr. Hano, who is already waiting for me."

"This is an honorable task. I respect that you are so determined at your young age. In Daze-Stone City, however, there are different rules. Robbery and violence are ordinary, and sometimes people are even murdered. Human nature can be shameful sometimes. I've seen a lot in my life. I can offer you my pension for tonight where you can safely rest, have a good dinner and a breakfast. Tomorrow morning you can continue on your way. Dar-Lan is still more than a week's walking distance from here, directly behind Big Peaky Mountain."

The sympathetic lady took the amazed Chon to the pension, ordered the manager to take care of him, then she left. The boy took over the room, then washed himself with heated, clean water from a wooden barrel in a public bathroom. After that, he ate all the food prepared for him with a massive appetite. It was overwhelming to feel that never-before-experienced comfort. He started to look at the walnuts in the corner of his room scornfully.

"Why do I have to carry this enormous burden?" he thought. "Many people live here in this city carefree, without carrying any burden on their backs. Most of them are not working at all, they just walk from one tavern to the next; they drink something, have a good chat with others, then move forward happily. Others live in even greater comfort, for example the owner of this pension. The whole city knows her, people tip their hats when they meet her on the street, and they follow her orders. And she does not carry any burden either. I want to live like that as well, have a bath each day in fresh and warm water, eat abundantly, and have people respect me."

Envy can often generate disturbing thoughts which can divert us from our mission. This is exactly what happened with Chon. His anxiety and curiosity to explore a new place would not let him rest. The more he thought, the more anxious he got. He went down to the common room and looked around. People were smoking cigars and playing cards, they were drinking and jovially chatting with one another. Suddenly, a smartly-dressed middle-aged man stepped up to Chon with a twisty grin.

"I saw you on the street. What forced you to bring that enormous bag with you alone to such a dangerous place as Daze-Stone City?"

"I am helping my family. I am taking the precious walnuts to sell, because we have to buy firewood for the winter."

"I see, my little friend. I can help you! I know a merchant in the city who would buy your walnuts for a good price, and he could even help you with the firewood."

Chon anxiously analyzed the situation. What could be the trick in the story, how could they cheat him, how would his father react if he did not follow his request? On the other hand, he was also considering that this deal could bring him extra recognition from his father for his vigilance in recognizing a good deal. But he was young and inexperienced. He did not know what the pitfalls of such a case could be. The cunning man, seeing his desperate speculation, continued:

"Maybe we can even discuss with the merchant a way to deliver the firewood directly to your farm, so you do not have to walk anymore, and you can make your father proud."

Suddenly from deep inside, Chon heard a voice which silenced for a short while all the other thoughts in his brain, like an eagle shoos the rabbits on a field when he appears in the sky. "If you deviate from the road, you can't get back before winter, and you will freeze, as will we." Then the firm voice disappeared, and all the scrum of the other thoughts took over its place again. To stop the endless inner monologue and to obviate the risk of the unforeseeable outcome of the deal, Chon firmly shook his head and said decisively:

"Thank you for the offer, sir, but I can only give the walnuts to Mr. Hano, who lives in Dar-Lan province!"

Then without waiting for the answer, he stormed out of the place, ran back to his room and locked his door.

The next morning, he set off early, but his legs advanced slowly. As he loaded the burden onto his back in the chilly autumn morning, he started to hesitate again:

"I should not have said that to the man. I was so stupid to refuse such a good offer. If I see that man again, I will surely accept his deal."

With similar thoughts in his head, he started to trudge slower and slower, while he felt the burden more heavily than before. But then suddenly he glimpsed Big Peaky Mountain and noticed that it was again closer than before. "It is just ahead of me," he thought, and this recognition saturated him with a sense of satisfaction that he had already progressed so far. He started to understand that Daze-Stone City was nothing but a new test, which he had completed successfully thanks to his consciousness. He felt happy and self-confident, which doubled his sense of power. In an hour he was already out of the city.

CHAPTER IV – THE TRIAL OF HEART

He advanced on the peaceful gravel road lined with trees. Beyond the trees there were meadows as far as he could see. The peasants were just sowing the crops for the next year. Chon was joyful that he was again in nature, which he already knew and where he moved more comfortably. He progressed quickly but at around noon he had to sit against the trunk of a tree to begin the humble lunch which he had taken from the pension. He put the bag of walnuts next to him. Suddenly his little bird-friend alighted on one of the branches just above the boy.

"Welcome back my dear little friend! Where were you?" asked Chon, but the bird just continued vivaciously singing. The boy smiled and was relieved to see the colorful bird again. Chon looked around, satisfied, and proudly noted that so far he had done a very good job. Not much further along, some peasants were having their breakfast too. They were sitting directly in the meadow not too far from the road, under the faintly shining autumn sun. It must have been an exceptional occasion because it seemed to Chon that most of the family was present for the lunch.

"Maybe the women have just brought the food for their men, or they might be celebrating something, and that is why they all gathered – Who knows?"

Suddenly he noticed a girl in the group of people. Although she must have been very young, she had already-mature features. She radiated vitality and joy, given to her by Mother Nature. She had long, thick, jet-black braided hair, which she sometimes tossed rakishly. Chon was somehow ashamed, but he could not take his eyes off the girl. He was enchanted. Her smile, her movements and her flickering eyes mesmerized him. When he looked at her, he was shocked in a way he had never felt before and his body was shivering. He continued his lunch, but his thoughts were going in circles. "I wish I could start a conversation with her," he sighed. He sized up his opportunities, but nothing seemed to be workable. "I cannot just walk over there and ask her about…something. What would they think?" he mused, sadly bemoaning his chances – as his little companion above him sang even more loudly.

"It is stupid. I would make an idiot out of myself. I will just simply forget this and continue my task as if nothing has happened. I have a much more important mission!"

He repeatedly looked in her direction, however, as if hoping for a miracle that would bring them closer to each other. Finally, their eyes met for a slightly-longer instant than before. His mouth became parched, his hands and legs started to tremble, and his heart beat as if his life depended on her. He was looking at an angel.

As time passed rapidly, the boy realized that he could not wait there any longer. His lunch was long finished, and he had to complete the last part of his mission. So, he reasserted himself and set off, coping again with the difficult emotions in his heart. His thoughts were far away. "I wish I could see her again, just to ask her name, which I would remember for my entire life." Somewhere deep inside, he hoped that they would see each other again.

As he was trudging along, sunk in his thoughts, he heard a cart approaching on the road. He stepped toward the side of the road to give priority to the vehicle, but when he turned back,

he thought that his eyes deceived him. On the cart among five or six other women, older and younger, he noticed Her! Yes, HER!! His little colourful friend, the bird, was flying from one branch to another in front of the cart – then suddenly it flew away up into the sky. As if a miracle had just come to pass, thus, he already had no doubt that he would end up on that cart, whatever happened. So, he started to drag himself quite obviously in order to look extremely tired and miserable. It was impossible that his unfortunate situation would not force the women to stop and help him.

Of course, they picked him up, and he ended up directly next to the charming little angel. She did not say anything to him, just continued talking with her friends, but in the meantime, she occasionally glanced teasingly at Chon, who bore the miracle spellbound. It was already late in the evening when they arrived home at a farm-stead which consisted only of a few houses with thatched roofs, connected to the country roads. As far as the eye could see, there were meadows and farm-steads similar to that where they had just arrived. Because night was already falling, the good peasants asked Chon whether he would like to spend the night there, and they offered him a comfortable place to sleep.

Although it was only in the barn, on the hay, he had never been so excited. Of course, the boy nodded. He thought that a fairytale had just come true. He felt it even more strongly when he looked into the sparkling eyes of the angel. He then took his place in the barn, he got a blanket, and not much later, the jet-black-haired girl appeared with some slices of bread and cheese and a glass of milk.

"Thank you!" said Chon, smiling.

"It is a pleasure for me that you spend the night with us. We do not have guests here often My name is Shira. What is your name?"

"My name is Chon, and I live in a farm twenty days' walk from here. My father sent me to Dar-Lan province to sell our walnuts."

They had an animated chat, their eyes sparkling, and they slipped into a different dimension, where time and space dissolved around them in a sweet harmony. The girl did not take her eyes off Chon, and occasionally laughed without warning. Every once in a while, when she said something, she touched Chon's shoulder or arm for emphasis. Eventually, much too soon, she said that she had to leave because she would be punished if she did not get back in time. Hesitating a little, she kissed Chon, then ran out of the barn. The boy did not regain consciousness for a while. He was overwhelmed by euphoric joy, but he was puzzled at the same time, not knowing what to do to see her again. As soon as he was able to think again, he did not want anything other than to see her once more. The bag of walnuts shrank down to a negligibly small detail, which did not matter anymore.

It was already pitch-dark outside. The stars were sparkling wanly. He stuck his head out of the barn, but there was nothing to see. An eerie calm and stillness ruled. His heart was beating wildly, but he couldn't allow his fear to stop him. He stepped out, looked around, and tried to find out where Shira might live. Nothing gave him the faintest idea. He trudged around the houses like a ghost. Suddenly the immense contour of a peasant blocked the stars in front of him. From his features, he might have been the father of Shira, and when he started to speak, it was already certain.

"I know what you are up to, you bloody maggot. Go back to your damn barn, and before dawn, get off my bloody farm, because I will not be this nice with you if I see you again!" he snarled, hurling Chon to the ground – then turned back and disappeared into a house.

Chon felt tragically ashamed while he crawled back to the barn and curled up on the hay next to his bag full of walnuts, his ever-reliable companion on this journey. He felt an awful remorse, even though he did not know what sin he had committed.

He did not sleep for a single minute. He tossed and turned all night, and the more he thought about what had happened, the less he understood. Before sunrise he set off with a deep sorrow in his heart. The strict father had made it easier for Chon to leave the place; he felt hopeless. He proceeded slowly and feebly. He felt that every step distanced him from his happiness.

CHAPTER V – RETURNING HOME

Not much later he reached Big Peaky Mountain which he had to cross to reach his destination. The mountain reached so high into the sky that some of its summit was already covered with snow on this autumn afternoon. From the heights, crystal clear water fell in waterfalls and fast creeks, which then were turned into rivers flowing on the timeless and eternal plains around the mountain. The gravelly road was accompanied by white rocks, deep ravines and steep cliffs all around. The air was pure and slightly pine-scented. Everything reflected the beauty and perfection of nature. Chon suddenly understood that the previous night, he had completed a new test again. He had managed to stay focused on his task and his consciousness had triumphed. He now felt happy, self-confident and satisfied.

Before he climbed too high, he decided that he would rest and only set off for the difficult terrain the next day. He made a fire and sank deep into his thoughts. In the meantime, the eerie shadows of the pines danced in the background.

Chon did not feel fear anymore. Three weeks of continuous trouble and fighting had made him tough. His muscles had hardened, and his endurance had significantly improved. Consequently, he could now carry the burden on his back for an entire day without being overly tired by nightfall.

He had cultivated an outstanding focus with which he managed to continuously concentrate on the success of his mission. He did not diverge from the path, did not rest more than necessary, and did not let his negative thoughts take control. His emotions had also stabilized. The self-confidence resulting from the recent weeks' successes gave him joy and more determination to make further progress. He started to feel an enormous power sprouting from a profound depth inside him, pushing him forward. This would not have been enough, though, to help him complete his task if he had not also been convinced that one day he would see Shira again. He could not explain how and when, but somehow he felt that the power of their love would be enough to bring them together again. This notion gave him an overwhelming sense of power.

He got up early the next day. The first rays of the sun had not illuminated the foggy valleys yet, but it was already possible to see. He washed himself in an ice-cold creek, then set off. The road steeply ascended. As the fog faded from the valleys following the sunrise, Chon's thoughts became clearer too. The beautiful environment amazed him, and he found an incredible joy in his task. He was not preoccupied with such details as how he would find Mr. Hano, whom he had never seen, because he was not anxious anymore about the success of his mission. His practiced consciousness had ripened and forged his awareness into a developed instinct which maneuvered him on his way with precision. He knew that he was on the right path, and that was all that mattered. He was in the present moment, fully concentrated. As he became entirely submerged in his mission and all his focus was on his task, he experienced a profound unity with the natural world around him, and this resulted in a deep satisfaction. The feeling was similar to the one he had felt when he was looking into Shira's eyes, seeing an angel in her. As he walked on the road, he smiled, and his legs took him automatically towards his goal.

In a few days he arrived in Dar-Lan into the village of Mr. Hano, and after asking a few questions from the friendly people on the street, he easily found his contact.

"Welcome to my village, young man! I knew that you would make this journey, and I am gratified to meet you personally," greeted Mr. Hano.

"Good afternoon sir!" answered Chon humbly.

"I believe, little man, that your journey was full of challenge, but you have managed to accomplish it well, and that is the most important thing," added Mr. Hano with a wide smile.

"It was the biggest adventure of my life. It seems that I have been on this journey for years, and actually I only left my farm 30 days ago, exactly."

"Time is relative, my dear little friend. It can be long or short, and if you are perfectly aware, in one moment you can find all of eternity." The man's eyes sparkled knowingly. Eventually, he paid the boy according to his father's promise, then Chon returned to his farm the next day in the early morning; the place where he'd set off four weeks earlier. The return was much easier without the burden, and the joy resulting from his successfully completed task multiplied his sense of power. He could hardly wait to get back home again and proudly hand over the money to his father to help him to buy firewood for the winter.

When he arrived home, his parents and his sisters warmly greeted him. His mother hugged him proudly with tears in her eyes, and his older sisters told him that from that moment onwards he would also be treated as an adult, because he was also a responsible part of the family.

He gave the money to his father who patted him on the shoulder, smiling genuinely. Chon could hardly bear to ask:

"My father, the barn is full of firewood for the winter. Why did we need the money if it was not to buy the firewood? Was my sacrifice for the family completely unnecessary?"

"Chon, my dear son, bravest of all, please sit down. I have to tell you something. This journey was not a simple journey. It was a test of majority. Each of your brothers had to undertake the same mission to justify their readiness for life. This has been a tradition in our family for hundreds of years and we have to keep it a secret from the following generations who will also have to do the same test."

Chon's jaw dropped as he heard those words, and he could not find the right response due to his astonishment. Then his father continued:

"As soon as you left, thus, we procured the firewood. This test was for your own development, and I knew that you could complete it. You could have backed off at the beginning. You could have lost the walnuts or sold them earlier. Walnuts can be sold in closer cities as well, for good money. But opposing all temptation to diverge from it, you continued your mission, sacrificing your short-term wishes for a higher purpose. This sacrifice made you stronger, smarter and more enduring. That small amount of money you received for the walnuts is negligible compared to the lesson you have learnt from the journey."

Chon thought about this and understood the lesson. That night, the little bird which had accompanied him on his journey sat on the frame of his window. It chirped in satisfaction, then flew away into the endless, stellar heavens from where it probably arrived. Chon went to sleep with a smile on his face. He thought about Shira and the kiss she'd given him when they saw each other last. He had never felt so happy, self-confident and satisfied as on that evening. He knew that they would see each other again, and that there was a wonderful life ahead of him.

THE END

Made in the USA
Middletown, DE
12 December 2018